First published in 1996
by Macdonald Young Books

Text copyright © Emma Fischel 1996
Illustrations copyright © Anthony Lewis 1996

This edition re-issued in 2008 by Wayland

Wayland
338 Euston Road
London NW1 3BH

Wayland Australia
Level 17/207 Kent Street
Sydney, NSW 2000

British Library Cataloguing in Publication Data available

ISBN: 978 0 7502 5580 6

Printed in China

Wayland is a division of Hachette Children's Books,
an Hachette Livre UK company

MY TEACHER THE GHOST

Emma Fischel

Illustrated by Anthony Lewis

WAYLAND

Chapter One

Dear Zoo

We think one of your wild animals has eksaped. It is ~~maskarading~~ ~~makserading~~ pretending to be a teacher in our shcool. Would you like it back? Its name is Mr Crabbe.

Yours sinserly

Joseph Ryan and Gemma Fairchild

Aged 7

Marvale School

Joey and Gemma had written that nearly two years ago. Not much had changed since then. They were still friends. Some weeks anyway. They still went to Marvale School, a stone's throw from Marvale Zoo. On a good day you could see the giraffes from the school playground. On a bad day you could smell the elephants from anywhere.

And Crabbo was still the pits. Mean and miserable, always snarling, always on the look-out for someone to pick on.

So no one exactly bawled their eyes after The Accident. A freak, one in a million kind of accident that lost Crabbo to the classroom forever.

It was all down to a case of him being in the wrong place at the wrong time. Being in the staffroom just as Daffodil, the hippo from Marvale Zoo, was being winched overhead, to be precise.

Daffodil was *en route* to the vet's for emergency surgery. She didn't much take to crane travel. She began to panic.

The crane began to buckle under the strain of one and a half tons of struggling hippo. The whole thing collapsed over Marvale School.

Poor Daffodil plummeted through the staff room roof and landed smack on top of Crabbo. He never stood a chance. He was flatter than a pancake in less than a second.

Daffodil was all right, though.

The next week, a supply teacher took over Crabbo's class. Miss Someone-or-other and grim as anything.

She spent the best part of the first lesson flicking through their workbooks. Tut, tut, tut, she muttered under her breath, with her mouth all puckered up like she had a lemon tucked in each cheek.

Joey sketched a robot on his pencil case. Anyone would think she'd never seen a marmite stain before, the way she was glaring at his science book.

Brrrr! He shivered like mad. The air had turned icy cold around him all of a sudden. He rubbed his arms. He felt as if he was packed in ice cubes. It was cold as the Arctic in here, which was odd because today was a real sizzler.

Joey frowned. Was he sickening for a rare disease? Or was it something the dinner ladies had put in the fish cakes?

Chapter Two

Rrring! The bell rang and Joey was first out of his seat. He shot out into the sunshine.

He sniffed, then coughed. An awful smell was wafting past his nose. He sniffed again. Whatever it was, it stank to high heaven. Like cabbage boiled in cough medicine, or mothballs fried in garlic. Worse than that, even.

He looked around.
No one else seemed to
have noticed anything.
Strange. Very strange.

All at once, the hairs on the back of his
neck started to prickle. Someone was
standing right behind him. Someone
with icy cold
breath.

He spun round.
There was no one
there.

Joey felt his
insides lurch.
What was going
on here?
Whatever it was,
he wanted it to
stop. Now.

"Hi Joey," said
a voice behind
him. Gemma!

Joey braced himself. This was a deadly enemies week. But Gemma, it seemed, was ready to bury the hatchet.

"Want to borrow my new Gurglers CD?" she said.

Beaming, Joey reached out to take it.

Whoosh! It whizzed up into the air before he had done more than touch it. It felt as if someone had whipped it out of his hand. But there was no one else near them.

The CD spiralled
through the sky, way
above them. Joey gaped.
He could never have
thrown it that far if he'd
tried. Which he hadn't.

It curved through a graceful arc above
the playground. Over the year ones
practising their skipping ... over the year
threes having a bust-up ... over the wall
... and smack under the wheels of a
passing bus.

Gemma turned to look at Joey accusingly.

"I-I didn't ..." said Joey, confused. But she was already stalking off. Miserably, Joey watched her stomp off out of the school gates. Then he trudged home.

The house was silent when he let himself in. No one was there. Just a note from his Dad propped up on the kettle.

Back later. Tea in oven.

Later, thought Joey uneasily. How much later? He flopped down in a chair and switched the telly on. It switched itself off.

Joey blinked. His heart started to beat a bit faster. He put on a video. It ejected itself. Well, more like hurled itself across the room and against the wall.

He felt cold inside. Go away, he whispered. Whoever you are, whatever you are, go away. Leave me alone.

All evening he was quiet as a mouse. Edgy, jittery, looking over his shoulder all the time. Something was going on that he couldn't explain.

Chapter Three

Lying in his bed that night, every little thing made Joey jump. The stairs creaking outside his room. The breeze whispering in the garden. The branches of the apple tree tap-tapping at his window. Familiar noises, everyday sounds; but they all made him pull the bedclothes closer and closer around him.

 At last he dropped off –
but in the middle of the
night he woke up again. Or
rather, something woke
him.

Flip, flip, flip.

What was it? His flesh turned clammy
with fear. One by one, the hairs on the
back of his neck stood on end. An icy
wind was moaning softly round and
round the room – but the window was
shut tight.

Joey started to
shake. Even
though the
bedclothes were
bundled tightly
round him, the
cold seeped
slowly into his bones. And all the while,
that strange noise came from the corner.
Flip, flip, flip.

Trembling, he rolled over. The pages of his exercise book were flipping over and over on his desk. His maths exercise book. But he hadn't put it there. He knew he hadn't put it there.

Now a smell was creeping into the room. A smell of rotting fish and old fruit left to decay in dark rooms.

Then Joey heard something else.
Scratch, scratch, scratch.
Scratch.

He couldn't move a muscle.

An ice cold breath brushed the back of his neck again. His heart started to pound. His teeth clattered with fear. Someone was here. Here in his room. He knew it. He could just feel it.

He lay awake, terrified and shivering, until the first light of dawn lit up the sky. Only then did he sleep.

Chapter Four

Joey made his way down the garden
path. He gave a big yawn. Tired he
might be, but at least he wasn't scared
witless now. Things seemed a lot better,
somehow, in the bright light of day than
in the darkness of the night.

Down at the bottom of the path he saw
Lofty, next door's poodle, hanging over
the fence. Joey hurried towards him.
They were old friends. But not today.

The moment Lofty saw Joey, he started to snarl. A low quiet snarl, deep in his throat. A terrified snarl. A snarl that said don't you come near me. He backed away, crouching low. His hackles rose. He bared his teeth. Then he turned tail and ran.

Joey clutched on to the fence. What was up with Lofty? He had seemed scared to death.

It was the same story everywhere. With the school rabbit, the school cat and all the gerbils in the science room. Every single one went into a flat spin when Joey came near. Whiskers all a-quiver, noses twitching and little feet taking them off in the opposite direction as fast as possible.

To top it all, Miss Whatsername had a word or two to say about his maths homework.

"Joseph Ryan," she said, glaring round the classroom. He looked up. She beckoned him to the front desk, pale eyes glinting coldly behind her spectacles.

Joey was baffled. He'd done his homework, after all. It might be wrong, but it was done.

"Explain this," she glowered, holding out his maths book.

Joey's mouth dropped open with shock. There was something scrawled across his homework.

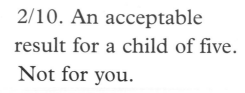

2/10. An acceptable result for a child of five. Not for you.

The thin scratchy writing wriggled across the page, faint and spidery, as if it had been written by someone with hardly the strength to hold the pen.

Scratchy writing. Thin scratchy writing. Scratch, scratch, scratch.

Joey thought back to last night – to the sounds in his bedroom, to the feeling that someone was there. A horrible suspicion was forming in his head. He had nothing to say.

But Miss Thingy did. In fact, she had quite a speech.

"Rarely have I known a child so keen that they not only do their homework," she said, one eyebrow raised so it peeked over the rim of her spectacles, "but take it upon themselves to mark it too. Such diligence shall be rewarded."

She smiled. Joey wasn't fooled. There was a nasty glint in her pale grey eyes. "See me at dinner-time," she snapped.

Chapter Five

They were very big sums indeed, the
ones Miss had set. Joey picked up his
pen and struggled to concentrate. It was
no good. The pen dropped out of his
shaking hand and clattered on to the
table. Question after question was
pounding round his brain.

What's going on? said a voice in his
head. Why is all this happening to me?
And, most of all, whispered the voice,
what happens next?

Joey shivered. Something was brewing, something truly terrifying. He knew it. He could just feel it …

Noises from the playground were floating in through the window. Yells, shrieks, snatches of songs – and Gemma's voice shouting louder than anyone's.

But inside the classroom, there wasn't a sound. Not so much as the tick of a clock or the scrape of chalk on a blackboard. There was just Joey, sitting alone in the silence.

Creak, crrrrk, crrrrk, crrrrk.

Over in the corner, the class hamster started to scrabble frantically round and round on its little wheel, whiskers quivering with fear.

The room went cold as the grave. A smell crept across the floor. A horrible smell. A smell of dead things. Of rotting things. Of decay.

A cold, cold breath drifted across the back of Joey's neck. Someone was in the

room. Someone was looking over his shoulder. Then he heard a little dry cough.

I know that cough, thought Joey, rigid with fear. I'd know that cough anywhere.

His eyes darted left and right. There was no one here. No one that he could see … Then he heard a sighing noise. A heavy sigh, a sigh of exasperation. And another little cough.

"Two out of ten," whispered a thin voice, cold as icicles. "Very poor show indeed."

Joey couldn't move, couldn't speak. This, without a doubt, was the most terrifying moment of his life.

"Even you," hissed the voice, "can work out that means eight wrong answers."

It was an ugly voice, nastier than nails scraped down a blackboard, crueller than the taunts of the playground bully. A voice that chilled Joey to the bone. And, worst of all, a voice he recognized.

It can't be, thought Joey … but in his heart he knew that it was.

"From now on," whispered the voice, "I shall haunt you. Day and night."

Chapter Six

Joey started to sway. Blind terror, blind panic, were welling up inside him. "Wh-wh-why? Why me?" he croaked.

"Because," hissed the cold, cold voice in his ear. "I was marking your homework when I unexpectedly departed this world. Your education is not yet complete."

Joey stood up, speechless with terror.

"You can never escape me," the voice continued. "Never!"

Joey backed away. "Go away!" he whispered. "Leave me alone."

Then he turned and bolted for the classroom door. He didn't know where he was going – but anywhere was better than here.

Click. The key in the door turned and locked all by itself. Joey rattled the key backwards and forwards in the lock. It wouldn't budge.

"Too late!" cried the voice in his ear with an evil giggle.

"Let me out of here!" Joey shrieked. He tugged at the door handle. He pounded on the door with his fists. It was no use.

He backed away towards the window. Cold slimy fingers, fingers colder than ice and slimier than worms, wrapped themselves round his left ear.

"Now," hissed the cruel voice in his ear. "Let lessons begin!" And for one brief instant the evil face of Mr Crabbe shimmered in the air. Green and glowing, gloating with pleasure. Growing closer … and closer.

Joey screamed.

"Leave!" ordered a voice. "Go from this place at once!"

Joey whipped round. Miss Thingy was standing by the door, pointing her long bony finger at the ghost. Her pale grey eyes were set in a steely stare.

The glowing green face of Mr Crabbe's ghost started to snarl. Its eyes glowed brighter then paler, brighter then paler. It gnashed its teeth. It spat with rage. And then it just faded away ... until it was gone completely.

Joey slumped with relief. Saved!
And it was all down to Miss Thingy.
Joey turned to thank her. Then he froze.
Wait a moment, he thought. The door
was locked. I know it was.
Locked from the inside.
So how? ...

Joey stared into the
pale unblinking eyes of
Miss Thingy. He
gulped.

"Only one per building," she said briskly. "That's regulations. And I was here first."

"Besides which," she added, "he's the sort who gives us all a bad name." Then her pale eyes began to twinkle. She winked a big pale wink.

Joey watched, open-mouthed, as Miss Thingy floated off through the classroom door in search of new paint pots.

Look out for more creepy titles in the Tremors series:

The Curse of the Ghost Horse by Anthony Masters

Jake believes the ghost tale of Black Bess, a horse that fell to her death shen forced tojump a huge crevasse. He is convinced the ghost horse is cursing his family and is determined to jump the crevasse to find Black Bess. But will Jake's obsession lead to his death...?

The Headmaster's Ghost by Sam Godwin

It's the school trip to Mortimer Hall. Adam and Melissa decide to scare Danny senseless by telling him the story of the evil headmaster's ghost who haunts the house. Danny is determined to show he isn't scared. But does his determination bring him more than he bargained for...?

Terror in the Attic by Barbara Mitchelhill

A lodger his rented the attic in Craig and Kelly's house, but there is something odd about him. Why does he always dress in black? What is in his leather bag? Desperate to solve the mystery of this stranger they decide to explore the attic. But does their curiosity get the better of them...?

For all these books and many more in the series Tremors contact:
The Sales Department, Hachette Children's Books, 338 Euston Road, London NW1 3BH